This Boxer Books paperback belongs to

. . . .

www.boxerbooks.com

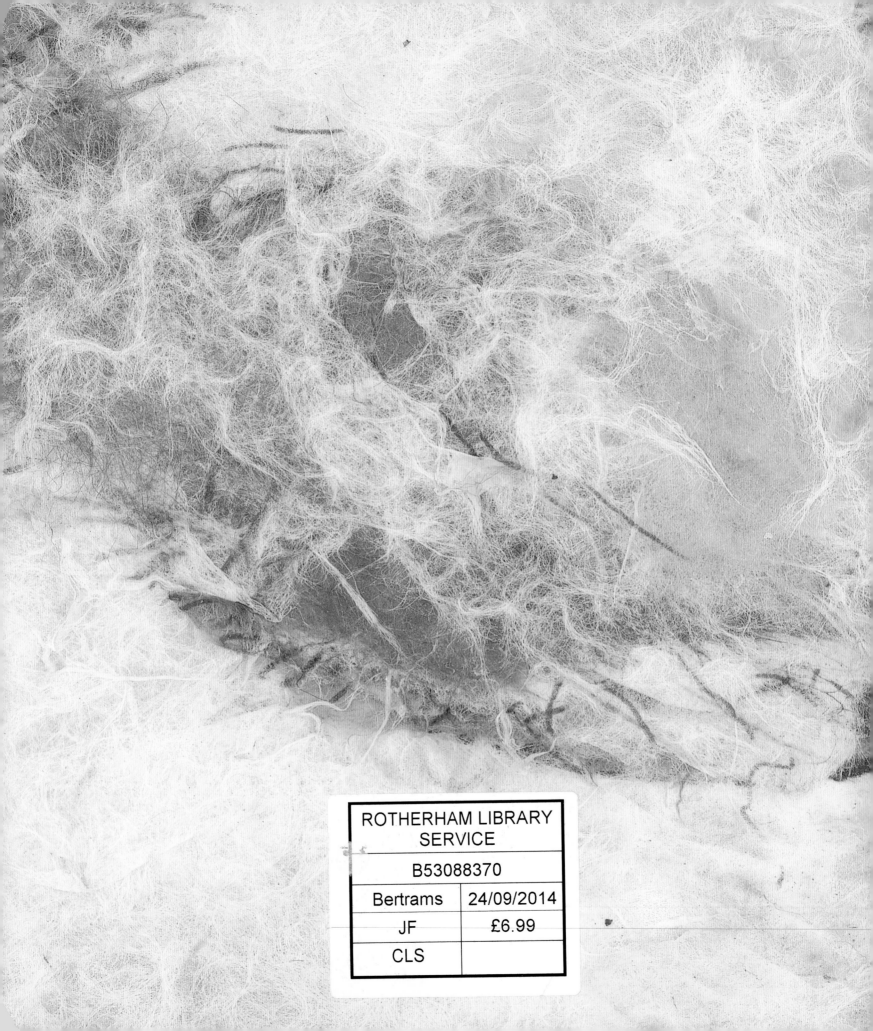

Good Luck, Baby Owls

Written by **Giles Milton**

Illustrated by **Alexandra Milton**

Boxer Books

Frost-coated silence,
a chill winter's night.
All is quiet in the
big dark barn.

All is quiet
except for a squeak.
A *squeakity-squeak* in the
big dark barn.

"Daddy, Daddy, Daddy!"
squeak two baby owls.

"Please, please, Daddy, Daddy,
can we learn how to fly?"

"Not yet," says Daddy.
"You're far too small.
You must wait for the
spring when your wings
will be strong!"

"But look, Daddy, Daddy,"
squeak two baby owls.

"We can both flap our wings.
Oh, please can we fly?"

"You must eat all your food,"
says kind Daddy Owl. "You need
to be strong to fly to the sky."

Day after day and week after week, they eat and they stretch and they flap their small wings.

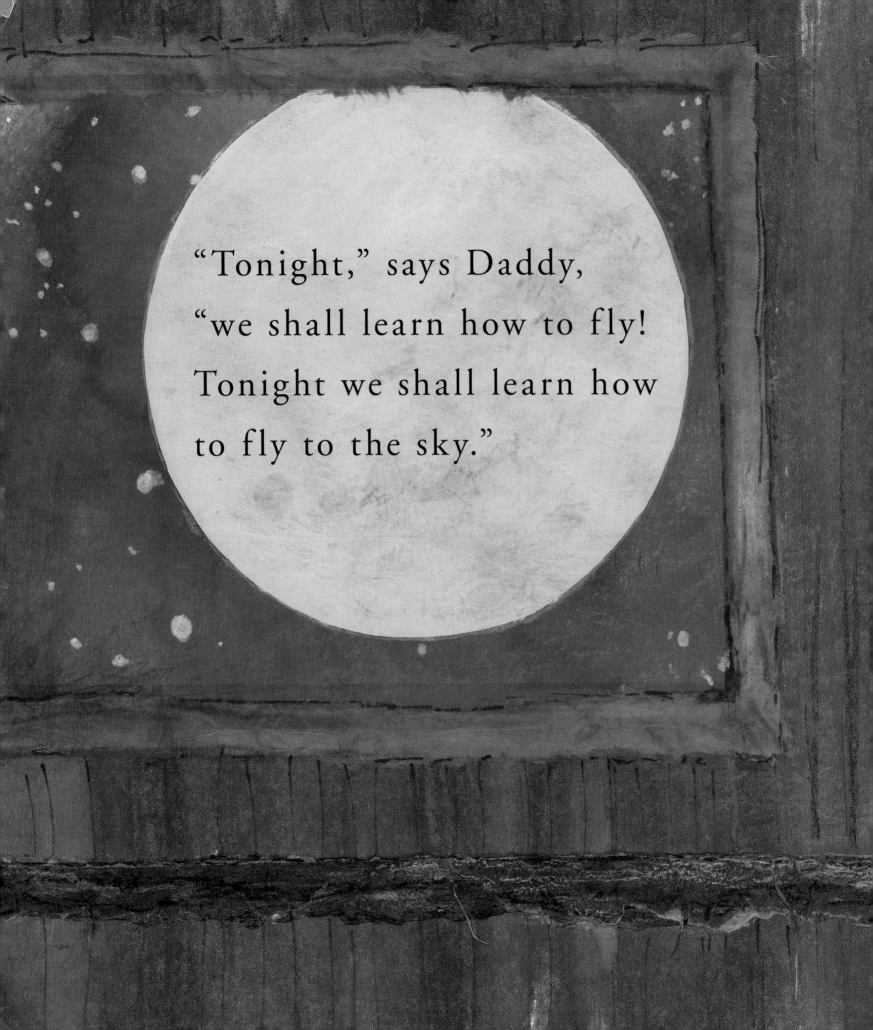

"Tonight," says Daddy,
"we shall learn how to fly!
Tonight we shall learn how
to fly to the sky."

High on a rafter sit two frightened owls.
Below, far below, is the far-away ground.

Above, far above, is the far-away sky.

"We're scared!" cry the owls.
"It's a long way to fall."

"Lean forward and flap,"
says strong Daddy Owl.

"We did it! We did it!
We learned how to fly!"
"I'm proud," says Daddy.
"So, how did it feel?"

"The sky is so empty,
so silent and clean ...
like floating in magic ...
can we do it again?"

"You can fly to the heavens,
you can fly to the moon.

Good luck, baby owls –
but fly back soon!"

For Philippe

G.M & A.M

First published in hardback in Great Britain in 2012 by Boxer Books Limited
First published in paperback in Great Britain in 2014 by Boxer Books Limited
www.boxerbooks.com

Boxer® is a registered trademark of Boxer Books Limited

The illustrations were prepared using collage, colour pencil and ink.

ISBN 978-1-907967-84-9

1 3 5 7 9 10 8 6 4 2

Printed in China

All of our papers are sourced from managed forests and renewable resources.

More wonderful animal stories
from Boxer Books - *Otter Moon* and *Tiger's Story*

Otter Moon
Written and illustrated by Tudor Humphries
Otter Moon is a beautifully illustrated tale of nature and adventure. Flibberty is a young otter who spends his nights on the riverbank, dreaming and staring at the moon. But one day, the King of the River gives him a task that takes him far away from home. As the moon rises over the river, Flibberty sets off on a journey towards the sea, trying to find a great fish and a silver dish before daybreak.

ISBN 978-1-907152-48-1

Tiger's Story
Written by Harriet Blackford
Illustrated by Manja Stojic
Tiger's Story follows the life of a young tiger cub, growing up in India. Simple text and striking illustrations combine to deliver non-fiction to a young audience with freshness, clarity and drama. Packed with facts and conservation information, this is a must-have book for every child. Tiger's Story was nominated for the Kate Greenaway Medal 2007.

ISBN 978-1-905417-42-1

The Art of Storytelling
www.boxerbooks.com